Winds of Time

Books in the *After Cilmeri* Series:
Daughter of Time (prequel)
Footsteps in Time (Book One)
Winds of Time
Prince of Time (Book Two)
Crossroads in Time (Book Three)
Children of Time (Book Four)
Exiles in Time
Castaways in Time
Ashes of Time
Warden of Time
Guardians of Time
Masters of Time

The Gareth and Gwen Medieval Mysteries:
The Bard's Daughter
The Good Knight
The Uninvited Guest
The Fourth Horseman
The Fallen Princess
The Unlikely Spy
The Lost Brother
The Renegade Merchant
The Unexpected Ally

The Lion of Wales Series:
Cold My Heart
The Oaken Door
Of Men and Dragons
A Long Cloud
Frost Against the Hilt

The Last Pendragon Saga:
The Last Pendragon
The Pendragon's Blade
Song of the Pendragon
The Pendragon's Quest
The Pendragon's Champions
Rise of the Pendragon

A Novella from the *After Cilmeri* Series

WINDS OF TIME

by

SARAH WOODBURY

Winds of Time
Copyright © 2012 by Sarah Woodbury

This is a work of fiction.

Cover image by Christine DeMaio-Rice at Flip City Books

To everyone who,
even for a moment,
wishes they could travel back in time ...

A Brief Guide to Welsh Pronunciation

c a hard 'c' sound (Cadfael)

ch a non-English sound as in Scottish 'ch' in 'loch' (Fychan)

dd a buzzy 'th' sound, as in 'there' (Ddu; Gwynedd)

f as in 'of' (Cadfael)

ff as in 'off' (Gruffydd)

g a hard 'g' sound, as in 'gas' (Goronwy)

l as in 'lamp' (Llywelyn)

ll a breathy /sh/ sound that does not occur in English (Llywelyn)

rh a breathy mix between 'r' and 'rh' that does not occur in English (Rhys)

th a softer sound than for 'dd,' as in 'thick' (Arthur)

u a short 'ih' sound (Gruffydd), or a long 'ee' sound (Cymru—pronounced 'kumree')

w as a consonant, it's an English 'w' (Llywelyn); as a vowel, an 'oo' sound (Bwlch)

y the only letter in which Welsh is not phonetic. It can be an 'ih' sound, as in 'Gwyn,' is often an 'uh' sound (Cymru), and at the end of the word is an 'ee' sound (thus, both Cymru—the modern word for Wales—and Cymry—the word for Wales in the Dark Ages—are pronounced 'kumree')

1

I wrapped my arms around my waist and leaned forward, trying to control my nausea as the plane shuddered and jerked. The pilot put out a hand to steady me, and then quickly moved it back to the controls.

"My God, Meg!" he said. "What just happened? We should be dead on that mountain! Now, I can't raise anyone on the radio—nothing but static—and I'm flying by the seat of my pants here. The electronics are good, but what I can see of the terrain looks totally wrong. I don't understand it!"

"Just put her down if you can, Marty," I said. "We can figure out what's going on when we land."

"Put her down? Where!" And then he screeched. The trees he'd been flying over gave way to a heavy sea, rolling beneath us.

"Jesus Christ!" Marty circled the plane back towards land.

I said nothing, just looked out the window at the country below, my chin in my hand. The fog was not as thick now, but it limited visibility to a quarter-mile. There were no houses or towns in sight and the land appeared rocky all the way down to the shoreline.

"Where in the hell are we?" Marty said.

As we were supposed to be flying over the mountains of Oregon right now, I could understand his bewilderment. I swallowed hard. The environment, if not the land itself, looked familiar to me.

The Middle Ages ... again.

I decided this fact wouldn't comfort Marty in the slightest.

"Fly south, Marty," I said, after he circled the plane for a third time.

I could make out the sun, trying to shine through the fog. It sat very high in the sky and made me think we were in the same late summer we'd left in Oregon, temporally anyway. Wild-eyed, Marty turned the plane as I had asked. We flew on, unspeaking. The land rolled away below us. The rocky coastline gave way to a hilly, grass-covered terrain, interspersed with stands of trees. Everything was beautifully green. The patches of ground we could see didn't include a city.

"We're going to run out of fuel soon," Marty said, his voice so quiet I almost couldn't hear him over the drone of the plane. "When that happens, what do you propose we do?"

I sighed. "Just put her down. Find a field. Hopefully people live among these trees, though I don't see any smoke."

"Smoke," Marty said. "I gather I'm not looking to follow the power lines?"

"I'm afraid there won't be any power lines."

"You do know where we are," Marty said. "What's going on here?"

I turned to look at him. "This has happened to me before," I said, enunciating as clearly as I could. "I can't explain it, but I'm afraid we've been displaced in space and time, to a world not our own."

Marty scoffed his disbelief. "You're kidding me!" Then, he looked through the windscreen at the pristine landscape over which we were flying. "You aren't kidding me?"

I shook my head, no happier with this new reality than Marty, but I'd come to terms with the possibility of it long ago. "Sixteen years ago, I lived in thirteenth century Wales for close to a year," I said. "I fear that we're back again, though whether in the same country or a different one, hundreds of years earlier or later, I don't know."

Marty gripped the yoke so hard his knuckles turned white. Just then, the fog thinned, revealing a small lake with a clearing next to it that looked like it could be a possible landing site. Without another word, Marty circled the little plane, lowering it to the ground as he did so. With only a few bumps in the grassy clearing, he landed and brought the plane to a halt. With a twist of his wrist, he turned off the engine, and we were quiet.

"I think I saw power lines to the north, just as we landed," he said.

"No, Marty. You didn't."

"I did. I know it."

I chose not to wait for further recriminations or questions I wasn't ready to answer, and wrenched the door handle. Pushing it open, I hopped out and hauled my backpack from the seat behind me. The lake lay a few yards to my right and was as clear as any I'd ever seen. Grasses grew almost to the water's edge, and wildflowers covered the hills around us. I took in a deep breath and gazed up at the sky, now as clear as the air I breathed. The fog was gone. *And what did that fog represent? The fog of confusion? The mists of time?* I had no answers for Marty.

Before we landed, I, too, had noticed something in the distance that looked manmade, though not power lines. Hoping to spot it again, I shouldered my pack and took off at a brisk walk, following the south side of the lake. After fifty yards or so, I angled away from the lake and headed up a small hill that formed the south side of the little valley. Another ten minutes of hard walking brought me to the top. I stopped and turned to look back at the plane, with Marty still seated inside. Then I gazed in the opposite direction and my heart skipped a beat. A long, stone wall stretched from east to west in front of me.

Dear God, it's Hadrian's wall.

I sagged to my knees. This was too much. It was bad enough to be in the Middle Ages again, but worse to find myself so far from Wales. I would have to cross miles of open country to reach Llywelyn, if he still lived in this world. Even if he'd changed the future as I'd urged, Llywelyn still might not have survived Cilmeri. The thought terrified me and hysterical laughter bubbled up in my throat. I tried hard never to think of him as a person, a human being whom I loved. I'd spent the last sixteen years studying his world, all the while pretending to know much less of him than I really did.

My time with Llywelyn had taken on the quality of a dream. If not for the very real existence of David, I could have told myself my journey to his time had never happened. That first meeting with Llywelyn occurred shortly after my husband's funeral. I lost control of my Honda Civic on a country road in the middle of winter, with Anna in the back seat. The road had been slippery and as I came to a stop sign, at the very place my husband had died, the car skidded sideways. Instead of hitting the hill that rose up beside the road, the car slid *through* it and into a marsh beside Criccieth Castle. I hit my head and had no memories until after Llywelyn rescued us.

I had been returned to my time at the moment of David's birth. He was Llywelyn's longed-for son, the one who would have ruled after him, had fate treated us differently. Anna had woken in the night and I had taken her to the toilet. I'd been squatting in front of her as she sat on the seat, her head resting on my shoulder, when my water broke. I gasped, and Anna gasped, and we were gone. We found ourselves in the grass outside my mother's house.

When my mother died a few years ago, I'd lost the one person who knew the truth about my life. I had always meant to tell David about his father, but it seemed needlessly cruel to fill him with stories about the other world in which he'd been conceived, but would never see. It would have made it impossible for him to fit into the twenty-first century.

With a flood of emotion, I realized that now I might be able to tell Llywelyn about his son—and just knowing that David existed, somewhere, might make a difference to him.

Too, it helped that I hadn't left Anna and David behind in the twenty-first century. Whatever the police investigators said, I didn't believe they were dead, or runaways, which is what the police assumed. It was too coincidental that they should vanish just as I had, very near to the place where I'd gone to Wales. I clung to the belief that they were still alive, but displaced to another world—like I was yet again. At the same time, if I dwelt on the idea at all, it terrified me not to know where they were. What if they made their way home again and found me gone? *My little girl … my wonderful son … please, God, take care of them.*

With these thoughts spinning in my head, I said a prayer for my mother, and for Llywelyn, and for my children, wherever they were, and stared out at the medieval landscape in front of me.

Thinking that it was time to talk to Marty, I turned around to head back to the plane and was astonished to see it rolling steadily across the grass. For half a second, I watched it dumbly. Surely, Marty wasn't going to take off and leave me here? Where exactly did he think he was going to go? Yet, I knew the answer without having to ask: to find his mythical power lines.

I shouted, though he couldn't hear me over the plane's engine, and then took off at a run down the hill. I had climbed too far, however, and I was only halfway down the slope when his front wheels lifted off the grass. Five seconds later, he was fifteen feet above the ground—then thirty—then one hundred. He circled the little plane around the lake and even had the gall to tilt his wings to wave at me, before heading north. I watched the plane's white tail until it disappeared.

* * * * *

"This is just terrific." I kicked a rock with my boot. "Stuck in the Middle Ages *again*! No proper clothing. No money. No food. In the middle of nowhere!"

I shouted my frustration to the sky as I paced beside Hadrian's Wall. I needed a plan and I needed it fast. At least it wasn't the middle of winter, so surviving alone in the open wasn't a problem. At least I hadn't landed in a packed church and been branded a witch. These were definite pluses.

In addition, I was no longer the ignorant girl I'd been when Llywelyn rescued me. In the subsequent years since my return to the modern world, I had raised my children with the help of my mother. I'd gotten myself back into college and eventually to graduate school. I had a Ph.D. in history, specializing (not surprisingly) in thirteenth century Wales. The last chapters of my dissertation, in fact, described what Wales *might have done* to avoid being conquered so completely by England. My dissertation committee hadn't liked that part of course—too speculative—but truth be told, that was where most of my energies had gone, and my interest had lain. If Llywelyn survived Cilmeri, I *needed* to get back to him. My whole being vibrated with the urgency of it.

Marty, in an apparent fit of remorse, had thrown my duffel bag out of the plane right before he took off. I had hauled it up the hill to my present location beside the Wall. I knelt in the grass to unzip both the duffel and the backpack to take inventory, and heaved a sigh at what I saw. I wasn't entirely without resources.

I had three or four changes of clothes, appropriate for summer wear, my makeup, manicure kit, and shampoo; a laptop computer with approximately four hours of battery life, assorted pens and paper, and my wallet; a small first aid kit in a metal tin, one package of M&M's, two maxi-pads, a comb, various assorted hair accessories, three paper clips, two safety pins, my cell phone, and a water bottle.

Furthermore, on my right hand I wore a ruby ring Llywelyn had given me, and in a secret pocket of my suitcase lay my late husband's diamond engagement ring on a silver chain. I'd kept it with me all these years, more in memory of Anna—the one good thing I'd gotten out of that relationship—than because of him. I would sell the diamond if I had to. Even if I were starving, I wouldn't part with Llywelyn's gift.

I sorted through my clothes. I had a broomstick skirt and a blouse that might be useful. I rolled them up tightly and put them in the bottom of my backpack, along with all my underwear, two pairs of socks—I loved cotton socks and, crazily, couldn't bear to part with them—and all the little items that might come in handy at some point. If anyone took a good look at what was in my backpack, I was going to the stake, but I would cross that bridge when I came to it.

Now what? I looked down at myself and hesitated over what to do. I wore slim khaki pants, a white t-shirt under a brown, suede jacket, and boots that matched the jacket. With a sudden thought, I rummaged through the leftovers that I'd dumped into the duffel and found a tweed cap Anna had thrown into the bag before that fateful trip to Philadelphia. After she disappeared, I couldn't bear to unpack it. I twisted my hair into a bun and pinned it to the top of my head by wrapping a couple of scrunchies around it and then pulled the cap on over the bun.

I tried to inspect the effect with the mirror in my make-up compact. Although everyone said that Anna and I looked alike, except for our hair and short stature, we really didn't. She was curvy and I had more of an athletic build. As much as I had once lamented that fact (particularly when I was sixteen years old and looked twelve), it could serve me well now. People see what they expect to see, and unless I called attention to the discrepancies, I hoped they'd think I was a boy.

I'd lived long enough in the thirteenth century to know that a boy had much more freedom of movement then a woman did. As a woman, I had no rights or status without a man to provide them for me, and it was rare, if not unheard of, for a woman to travel alone. When I had lived with Llywelyn, my status as his woman had sheltered me from the harshness of life in the Middle Ages. I had loved him so completely, I hadn't given much thought at the time to how different my experience would have been if a peasant had rescued me instead of the Prince of Wales.

Now at thirty-seven, with Llywelyn far away and unable to help me, I was more vulnerable than I had ever been in any world, past or future. As a woman, if strange men came upon me, I would have to rely on their honor not to harm me, or I would have to trade my body for protection. *If I was even given a choice in the matter.*

After burying the duffel as best I could under a bush near the Wall, I hoisted my pack onto my back. Convinced I had no real alternative, I straightened my shoulders, put my thoughts aside, and turned towards the west in the direction of Wales. I started walking.

My sole concern was to avoid meeting anyone. Fortunately, it was unlikely that any Scots would patrol this far south, since Hadrian's Wall was well into England and not a busy place in the thirteenth century, with few farms or villages. I didn't know where I was along it, but I figured that would become clear when I came to a guardhouse or settlement. I could see several miles in all directions, and momentarily content, I turned my thoughts to formulating some kind of plan. Unfortunately, nothing was coming to mind.

My future began and ended with Llywelyn. I couldn't bear the thought of living the rest of my life in this world without him. All my hopes centered on finding a way back to him.

2

I marched along the southern side of Hadrian's Wall, to the north of the road the Romans had built in order to connect their forts together and so they could better patrol their northern border. It was approaching nine o'clock when I reached the remains of a fort where I could rest for the night. I had passed the remains of fortlets which the Romans had placed every mile along the wall, but none felt secure enough to stay in. Besides, I wanted to walk as long as it was light.

My history told me that the major forts were six miles apart, but this was the first one I'd come to. Either I was walking more slowly than I'd thought, or I had missed one that wasn't actually attached to the wall or was so much a ruin I hadn't recognized it.

This fort was relatively intact, I was pleased to see, with the walls standing well above my head, still fifteen feet high. In the twenty-first century, this fort would be nearly two thousand years old and much decayed. Now, it was only a thousand years old and it made a difference to be here before that extra thousand years of weather and people pillaging the stones.

The darkness grew as I tried to find the entrance. I had never been much of a night person, and dawn came early to England in summer. Better to sleep now, if I could, than walk on until it got completely dark and find myself without shelter. I followed the wall of the fort as it jutted out perpendicular to Hadrian's Wall and walked some ways until it turned to head west again. I hadn't realized how big a three acre fort could be. I had only been to a small section of Hadrian's Wall before (in modern times), near Newcastle, and had learned then that the forts could hold more than a thousand men.

Finally, I reached the southern gateway and crossed the threshold into a large space. It was magnificent. A shiver went down my spine and I remembered again what it had been like that first time in Wales, traveling through the countryside with Llywelyn.

The fort stretched before me. A large courtyard was surrounded by smaller buildings, mostly wrecked. I headed towards those on the eastern side, looking for shelter so that

I could sleep, at least for a little while. I didn't believe that anyone would come to the fort so late at night—if they ever came at all—but I didn't want to be discovered if they did.

As with the Roman fort I'd passed through with Llywelyn (I really wasn't going to be able to keep him out of my head, was I?), one of the rooms at the fort contained an altar with a picture of a bull carved into the stone. Roman soldiers had worshipped Mithras here, as part of the secretive, all-male cult popular in the Roman legions.

I stood uncertainly in the doorway, surprised to see footprints in the dirt in front of the altar and a dark stain across the front of the stones, evident even in the failing light.

The stain looked like blood. Surely men didn't *still* worship here?

Christianity had taken over England long ago—but perhaps not everywhere. Perhaps a fringe group found refuge here from time to time. I walked forward and ran my hand gently over the stone. The worship of Mithras had involved animal sacrifice, usually goats or sheep. *Please let this not be human blood!* No matter what had made the stain, it had long since dried. I was imagining things; perhaps the footprints were quite old and had remained undisturbed for many years. There was a roof over this section of the fort, so the outside weather would not have touched them.

I backed out of the room and made my way across the fort through the rubble to a different section. I settled upon a private space built into the western wall of the fort. It appeared to have once been a guard tower. It had a roof that would protect me from any sudden rain, though I wasn't concerned about the weather. As changeable as weather in England could be, stars glittered above my head, giving me enough light to see by.

I set my pack against the wall, sat down, and leaned against it. I unscrewed the cap to my water bottle and tilted all but the last inch into my mouth. I would need to find more water in the morning. Fortunately, there were many little streams and rivers near the Wall. As I'd walked earlier, I had gladly filled my bottle from them when I found them, hoping for the best in terms of sanitation. I assumed there would be more as I went along tomorrow.

Hadrian's Wall was only seventy-miles long, straddling the north of England with Newcastle in the east, and Carlisle in the west. Even if I was quite far east when I started, it couldn't be long before I would reach a settlement where I could find food. Two or three days without food, as long as I had water, would not kill me. I scrunched down further and rested my head against my backpack so I could stare up at the ceiling. I tried to relax my shoulders and empty my head of worries. It wasn't really possible, but after I counted several hundred sheep, I fell asleep.

* * * * *

I awoke to the sound of crying. Heart racing, I sat up. My ears strained to hear better. Then it came again, the distinct sound of a child weeping. I got to my feet, took a few steps into the center of the room, and then thought better of it. Instead of shouldering my pack, I stuffed it behind a fallen rock and took a moment to layer several smaller ones over it. It was the best I could do in the dark. I didn't want to risk a medieval person coming across it by mistake.

I hurried from the room, following the child's sounds and arrived in the main courtyard of the fort. The moon had risen while I'd slept, illuminating the stones. A young boy huddled with his back to the wall by the door.

I stopped short at the sight of him, truly stunned. What on earth could a child be doing here in the middle of the night? I glanced towards the room that held the altar, but no light appeared inside it and it seemed the boy was alone.

He looked up as I approached and held out both hands as if to push me away. "Don't hurt me!"

I stopped again. For all that I'd been working with medieval English (and medieval Welsh, of course) for the last ten years, it took me a second to register what he'd said and to orient my thoughts so that my words would come out right.

"It's all right," I said. "I won't harm you."

"Are you a ghost?"

So *that's* what he was thinking. Most medieval people avoided the Roman ruins because spirits might haunt them. "I am no spirit. Just a traveler like you."

"I'm not a traveler," the boy said, gaining courage. "I'm a squire!"

I closed the distance between us and crouched in front of him. The shadow of the wall obscured his face, but from his size, I guessed he was ten or twelve years old.

"You are young for such a big job," I said. "How did you end up here?"

"The Scots." The boy spat on the ground. "I rode out of Carlisle with one of my uncle's companies and we ran into—" The boy swallowed hard, unable to finish his sentence.

I touched his hand and was glad when he turned his palm face-up and allowed me to grasp it. "Did any of your uncle's men survive?"

The boy shook his head.

"Where are they now, the Scots I mean?"

"Riding north—or they were," the boy said. "They didn't tie my feet and I slipped off the back of the pack horse they'd thrown me over. This was before the moon was up. I ran here. I didn't see anyone follow."

"So they captured you? Only you?" I said.

He nodded. They'd wanted him for ransom, probably, recognizing the fine cut of his cloth and that he wore mail armor, even though he was just a boy. I was surprised the Scots had ridden this far south, and even more surprised his uncle hadn't ridden with him.

"What is your name?"

"Thomas Hartley. My uncle is Sir John de Falkes. He crusaded with King Edward and now guards his northern border against the Scots."

I caught my breath, my heart pounding. *I was close, so close! It could be 1284, it really could!* Hysterical laughter rose in my throat. I bent my head forward, glad that Thomas couldn't see my face any more than I could see his. He coughed under his breath but didn't comment. Maybe he thought I was crying.

Relieved that the boy wasn't in immediate danger, I cleared my throat. "Give me a moment. I need to gather my things. Then we'll start walking again. We need to get you to your uncle."

I left him by the front door and ran back to the side room, pulled out my pack, and once again dumped the contents on the ground. I pawed through them for anything small enough to fit into the pockets of the jacket I wore, which fortunately had inner as well as outer pockets.

The first aid kit went in first, followed by the ibuprofen, my nail clippers, safety pins, and two maxi-pads. I looked longingly at the socks, but put them back in the pack. The unusual clothing I wore was bad enough without adding to it.

Since I was going to be female from now on, I dropped the hat in the pack. I hurriedly combed out my hair and braided it ... and then stopped, still holding onto the thick plait with one hand. What to tie the end with? A scrunchie wouldn't do. They didn't have rubber bands in the Middle Ages. I rummaged in the pack and came up with a dark blue ribbon from the hem of the broomstick skirt. I cut a length of it with the scissors from the first aid kit.

Then I slipped the chain, on which my ex-husband's diamond ring was strung, around my neck, took off my watch (very reluctantly) and stowed it in the pack, which I put back behind the stones. There was no help for it. I couldn't keep it. I stacked a few more rocks to hide it better and mused that an archaeologist of the future was going to get a major surprise.

By the time I got back to Thomas, he was on his feet. He glanced at the moon. "I reckon it's after midnight now."

"You're probably right," I said. "Would you rather stay here until morning?"

"No!"

"So let's get walking."

Much cheered, Thomas led the way out of the fort and headed west on the southern side of the wall (so as to avoid any stray Scots). I followed, trying to keep a steady pace, but Thomas, who'd been sad and scared before, rather than injured, was irrepressible now that he had company. At one point he broke into a run. When I refused to keep up, he slowed and then stopped to wait for me.

"My uncle will be very worried about me," he said.

"How many men were in your company?" I said.

"Twelve, in addition to me." Thomas bit his lip.

"Was it your first scouting trip?"

Thomas nodded. It might be a long time before he was allowed out again.

The wall rose and fell to our right, following the hilly terrain. Neither Thomas nor I had any idea how far it might be to Carlisle. We walked for several hours, but some time before dawn, clouds blew in to cover the moon. I couldn't see see the dips and stones in the road any longer and stumbled twice on rocks before falling to my knees on a third impediment.

"We have to stop," I said.

Thomas gazed west, his hands folded on the top of his head and his eyes straining for any sign of the city. "It can't be much farther."

"It really could, Thomas. Let's rest until morning." A small stand of trees grew to our left. I eyed it, thinking it might provide enough shelter for us to pass what remained of the night. As soon as the sky began to lighten, we could set out under better conditions.

Reluctantly, Thomas allowed me to lead him across the fifty yards of grass to the trees. As we passed under them, their leaves obscured the moon and it was quite dark. Thomas found a tree that was free of brambles, and settled himself at its foot. Neither of us wore a cloak so I sat beside him and put my arm around his shoulders. He leaned into me, resting his head against my breast.

"I never asked your name," he said, after a minute.

I smiled. A ten year old's oversight. "You can call me Margaret."

"You speak strangely," the boy said.

"To me, you speak strangely too. I have never been here before and much of this land is unknown to me."

Thomas didn't reply and I thought he might have fallen asleep.

"Thank you for saving me," he said.

Within two minutes, his breath came slow and even.

I eased my back further down the tree so I didn't sit so upright and closed my eyes too. But I couldn't sleep. In the cold, dark woods, alone but for a ten year old boy, the fragility of my position pressed on me. I sat a little straighter again, opened my eyes again, and watched.

3

I awoke to find two boots next to my nose. One of them shifted to poke me in the ribs.

"Wake up!"

I could have sworn I had stayed awake the whole night, but just when I should have been watching, I must have fallen asleep. Isn't that always the way of it in the movies? Thomas still slept, cradled against my side. His weight prevented me from shifting so I could see the speaker. Instead, the owner of the boots crouched in front of me and I found myself looking into blue eyes and the stern face of a man of an age with me—middle thirties, maybe even younger.

"Allard." Blue-eyed man threw the words to the man behind him whose face I couldn't see. "You and Francis lift the boy and bring him to my horse. I will carry him home myself."

"Yes, Sir John."

Sir John kept his gaze steady on me as Allard and Francis raised Thomas up.

"He's not injured," I said.

Thomas yawned and rubbed his eyes. "Uncle!"

Sir John relented some of his sternness and grabbed Thomas up in a bear hug. For my part, I struggled to my feet, very conscious of my twenty-first century clothing. I clutched my short jacket closed and folded my arms across my chest. Sir John looked at me over the top of his nephew's head. "And you are?"

Thomas released his uncle enough to twist towards me. "This is Margaret, Uncle. She and I walked from the Roman fort together."

Sir John's eyes narrowed. "Which Roman fort?"

"Your nephew found himself alone and on the run from some Scots," I said. "He ended up at a fort along the wall."

"I might ask what you were doing there, dressed as you are." His eyes inspected me up and down. "But for now, we best be getting home." And just like that, he turned away from me and towards his horse, which he mounted on a single, fluid motion.

Thomas scampered after him. Sir John gave the boy his arm so that he could clamber up after him on the back of the horse. I had followed Thomas from the woods, but now backed away, thinking that continuing the journey by myself wasn't a bad idea. Sir John had a different notion, however.

"Francis!" Sir John jerked his head, directing Francis' attention towards me. Francis nodded. A moment later, I found myself grasped by the arm and urged towards Francis' horse. "Can you ride?"

I stared up at the beast and sighed. "Yes."

Sir John laughed. "Look after her, Francis. I have many questions." He spurred his horse away.

I hadn't ridden more than a few times since my year with Llywelyn, but I knew what to do. I grasped the horse's mane and Francis threw me up onto him. I swung my leg over the horse's back and tried to get comfortable. I closed my eyes. *Where will this end?* A second later, Francis mounted behind me. Perhaps he feared that I would slip off the back and run away if he didn't contain me.

I'd been fortunate so far that neither Thomas nor Sir John had pressed me about what *I* was doing at the wall. Sir John would corner me eventually, and if I couldn't get myself free first, I was going to have to come up with a satisfactory story with which to explain myself. I hated to lie and couldn't trust myself to lie convincingly anyway. My hope lay in finding a truth palatable enough for John, that was also true for me. *Hopeless.*

We set off at trot, which quickened to a ground eating canter. The sun had fully risen now and it promised to be a beautiful summer day.

It took us almost two hours to reach Carlisle Castle, Sir John's home, located within the city of Carlisle. As the castellan for Edward I, Sir John would be one of the men spearheading Edward's invasion of Scotland in another few years. Another bit of history that I would change if I could. I decided not to mention that to Sir John.

* * * * *

Once at the castle, Sir John arranged for a servant to lead me to the bathing room, located just off the kitchen. Discarded clothes that needed washing sat in baskets near a back exit that led to the large troughs where laundry was done. A fire warmed the room, which it needed, even though it was summer. It was England after all. The water for the bath was warm too and I made the most of it. Afterwards, the woman presented me with a linen shift and a dress of deep blue that matched my eyes perfectly.

I had no mirror but I could see something of my reflection in the basin. The servant rebraided my hair in two plaits (tying each with a leather thong), making me look far younger than my thirty-seven years. I shrugged. It would have to do. As my final preparation, I stacked my old clothes in a neat pile in a corner, along with all my goodies but the two rings, awaiting the moment I could collect them again.

I edged open the door to see if anyone was in the passage. It was empty. *Now it begins, and I am such a lousy liar.*

When I entered the great hall, it was full of people eating. I gulped. It had been a long time since I'd faced this kind of audience—in fact, it was the day after I fell into the past the first time, sixteen years ago. And that time, I had baby Anna on my hip.

Sir John sat at the head table, in the primary position, as was usually the case with lords in their own hall. Thinking of Llywelyn again, I squared my shoulders. I would find courage in his memory. *Best get on with it.*

At a signal from Sir John, I walked to him and came to a halt a pace away, on the other side of the table. I folded my hands and looked at him, aiming for an innocent and expectant expression. Now that I wore appropriate clothing, chances were better that I could *pass* for the medieval woman I was not.

"If it doesn't trouble you greatly," he said, "please break your fast in my receiving room. I have questions for you."

"Of course, my lord," I said.

He rose and I followed him from the room, through a doorway, up a small stairway to another room on the upper floor. The room was spacious and well lit with candles on the table and the window shutters thrown wide. Sunlight poured into the room from a west-facing window. Contrary to his promise, no food appeared and Sir John moved to stand before the fireplace. He prodded the lit logs with a poker.

"So, Mistress Margaret," he said to the flames, "you appear to be a most unusual woman. It is time to tell me of yourself."

I swallowed hard. "Myself?"

Sir John rested a forearm on the mantle and turned to look back at me. "Yes, Mistress. Yourself." Dry amusement filled his voice. "I await with great interest your explanation of what brought you to the Roman fort in time to help my nephew."

I had known that he would ask me this. I'd labored on a viable story during the ride to Carlisle and then in the bath, discarding tale after tale as ludicrous and unbelievable.

"Well then," he said after a long pause which I didn't fill. "We will start with your place of birth, Margaret. Who is your father and where does he live?"

I swallowed hard. A softball question, sort of, if one had a mind to tell the truth.

In the silence that followed, he seated himself in a throne-like chair that had been set before the fire. He rested his elbows on the arms of the chair, folded his hands together, and pressed the tips of his forefingers to his lips. He studied me for a while longer and then gestured that I should post myself in front of him, three paces away. It was like being sent to the principal in grade school.

I decided I couldn't postpone this conversation any longer. "My father is Bran ap Morgan, my lord, of Gwynedd."

"Of Gwynedd!" Sir John straightened and dropped his hands so that he gripped the arms of the chair. "Thus, the reason for your strange accent and your outrageous manner. It is said that the Welsh allow their women too much freedom and I believe it. And your grandfather?"

This was it, the first plunge into deep water. "On my mother's side, my grandfather was Goronwy ap Ednyfed

Fychan, the former seneschal to Prince Llywelyn, and the father of one of his current advisors, Tudur."

"Ah yes." Sir John sat back, looking satisfied. "You have explained much in only a few words, particularly your royal bearing and gait."

Stunned relief rushed through me, though not because of Sir John's satisfaction with my story. Rather, it was his acceptance of my use of the word 'current'. Llywelyn had a current advisor! *He is alive! My Llywelyn is alive!* The knowledge left me so weak at the knees I almost collapsed to the floor.

I wished I could run from the room and shout my joy to the sky, but instead I had to stand there and calmly answer Sir John questions. Anything else wasn't going to get me back to Wales.

Sir John gestured towards me with one hand. "Pray continue. It is a long way from Gwynedd to Carlisle, is it not?"

"Yes, my lord." I paused, marshalling my thoughts, but more confident now that I had hope for the future. "I spent the first fifteen years of my life at the court of Prince Llywelyn, under the guidance of my grandfather. But with Dafydd's betrayal of the Prince, my life changed. My father was killed in the fighting and my mother chose to leave

Wales and return to her mother's house, taking me with her. My grandfather was not married to my grandmother, you see, who was from Shrewsbury, on the Welsh border."

"Yes, I know it," Sir John replied. "I have accepted the hospitality of the Benedictine monks there."

"At the Abbey of St. Peter and St. Paul?" I asked, silently thanking Ellis Peters and her Brother Cadfael mysteries.

"Indeed," replied Sir John. "Pray continue."

"I had not lived in Shrewsbury long before I was married to an Englishman at my mother's insistence. She feared for my future were I to return to Wales, even though Llywelyn was crowned Prince of Wales around this time."

"He was crowned nearly twenty years ago," Sir John said.

"Yes, my lord," I said, wondering why he thought to comment on it. "I had a daughter, and then a son. Shortly after our son's birth, my husband began to change."

Sir John leaned forward. "Change in what way, Margaret?"

"He ... he began to turn away from the Church, my lord," I said, in a rush. "He began to leave the house at all hours and not return until dawn. It only happened a few times a year at first, and then every month, until ..." I stopped. I eyed Sir John carefully, but he seemed riveted.

"Until what?"

"Until he confessed to me his worship of Mithras." As I spoke, I inadvertently looked down at my feet. If Sir John had studied psychology he would have known that this indicated I was lying through my teeth.

"Ah, now we reach the heart of it. What then?"

"With Prince Llywelyn's recent victories ..." I paused to see how I was doing and found Sir John nodding. Before he noticed my clenched fists, I hurried to continue my story.

"My daughter and son are grown now and I could leave them. I sent them to the Prince's court. I, in turn, accompanied my husband to Newcastle-on-Tyne, where he insisted we could lodge with his great-aunt whom he hadn't seen in some time. When we arrived we found that she had died the previous year. We had no place to stay and little money. My husband paid an innkeeper for a few nights of meals and lodging for me, and disappeared with only the clothes on his back.

"I didn't know what to do when he failed to return. At last, I became determined to find him and make a final attempt to draw him away from these evil doers. I cut down some of his clothes for myself and, dressed as a man, set out to find the location of their worship. Over the years I had learned a little of their practices. I confess I listened to his private conversations with his companions when he thought I was asleep. I had learned that a night which promised both a full moon and a clear dawn would bring them out. I knew that the wall built by the Romans was the center of Mithras worship in England. Several days ago, I set out from Newcastle along the wall.

"When I encountered a fort and its altar to Mithras—not where I found your nephew, but a location further east—I realized I had reached the right place. I hid myself. This was two nights ago. I didn't have to wait long before men came, dressed in long white cloaks and hoods. My husband ..." I bent my head and bit my lip. I had really fallen down the rabbit hole here. "My husband was one of them. They were in the middle of the ritual when the Scots—perhaps the same ones who captured your nephew—rode out of the dark and killed them all."

"I am sorry for your loss, Margaret," Sir John said, not sounding sorry at all. "So you expect me to believe that you followed your husband to Newcastle, dressed yourself as a boy, walked along the wall for several days, hid yourself in the fort, witnessed a Scot raid, and then rescued my nephew."

"Yes, my lord," I said, my throat dry. "I do."

"The surprising thing," Sir John said, "is that I do believe you. I've known about the Mithras cult for some time and have tried to stamp it out in Carlisle. What makes me wonder, however, is why in all of this, you chose to lie about your age?"

I blinked. My age was the one thing—maybe the only thing—I absolutely had *not* lied about. "My age, my lord?"

"Yes." Sir John rose to his feet. He stood in front of me, his hands on his hips, and leaned down to look directly in my face. "Your age!"

He straightened and walked in a full circle around me. I looked towards the fire, uncertain.

"I do not believe for one moment that you are, what? Thirty-six or seven?" Sir John continued. "Do you think your woman's folly will be more easily excused if you mark your age as that of a grandmother, instead of the girl you are?"

Sir John stood in front of me once more. I averted my eyes and he smiled as he took my chin in his hand and made me look at him.

"Do you care to revise how old your children are, my dear? Perhaps you would like to mention that you went to Shrewsbury with your mother at Prince David's second defection, not his first. Even then, that would make you twenty-five." He turned my face from side to side, inspecting me. "That might be possible."

He released my chin and I returned my eyes to the floor. He sat in his chair again. Silence descended on the room. Finally, I decided that I had lied about everything else, I could lie about this too if it made Sir John happy and distracted him from the rather extensive falsehoods in the rest of my story.

I sighed. "My children are six and eight, my lord."

"Women's foolishness knows no bounds, apparently," Sir John said, a ring of satisfaction in his voice. "I do not know how you thought I would believe you had achieved such an age."

"I did not think, my lord." A fit of giggles threatened to overwhelm me. My shoulders began to shake from the effort of swallowing them.

"No need to cry, my dear," Sir John said. "You have experienced much in the last few days. Thank you for your care of my nephew. You may go."

Without another word, I turned from him and fled. I raced down the stairs and then down a second flight to the bathing room. I had a mind to leave Carlisle immediately. With all the comings and goings in the castle, I could hide among the general populace moving through the front gates and lose myself in the city.

I pulled up short as I entered the room. It had been completely cleaned and my clothes—and everything I'd secreted inside them—were gone. I closed the door behind me and leaned back against it. Resting my head against the door, I began to laugh—so hard I couldn't stop—until I really did begin to cry.

4

I lay on a pallet that night, in a room with several women of the court, worried that it might be a long time before I could figure out how to leave. I had no money or friends, no resources other than my former husband's diamond ring (the pawning of which might take some doing), and I hadn't been able to track down my few possessions. The maidservant I questioned only shrugged and said they'd been disposed of. *Great.*

The next evening at dinner, however, Sir John informed me that he was making arrangements for me to find lodgings at the nunnery of Armathwaite, seventeen miles southeast of Carlisle.

Startled, I focused on my food, trying to think how to respond. I hadn't anticipated this particular side effect of looking twelve years younger than my true age. Sir John was correct to send me away. Although women lived among his court, I had no guardian, no authority over me besides what he chose to wield. It made it impossible for me to stay at the castle for more than a few days.

"A nunnery?" I said.

"Yes, of course. It isn't far. You will leave in the morning—early, mind—and should arrive at the nunnery before noon. I will compensate the nuns for your keep until such a time as you are able to make your way south to Shrewsbury."

To Sir John, this was the perfect solution for me. The nuns wouldn't require me to take orders, but they would provide me a safe place to stay. He could ensure that I had the same shelter and food he was giving me, but without the hassle. That was all very well and good, but if I was to buy passage to Wales, I needed more than this. Thus, after the meal, I followed Sir John as he left the table. Pulling my the diamond ring from under my dress where it had been resting on the chain around my neck, I held it out to him.

"My lord, would it be possible to exchange this ring for gold to pay for my keep and passage south?"

Sir John glanced at my face and then gazed at the ring, though he didn't touch it.

"This ring is worth a great deal, Margaret," he said. "May I ask how you came by it?"

I had been reluctant to approach Sir John because I feared he would ask this question. The ring was modern, of course, but I'd dirtied it up a bit and I hoped it could *pass* for medieval more easily than I could. "It was a gift from my grandmother, before I set out to Newcastle with my husband. My grandfather had given it to her many years ago, but she gave it to me because she feared for me. I am loath to part with it for that reason, but I cannot be a burden to you."

Sir John shook his head. "My dear, you must keep it. I am in your debt for the life of my nephew. Without question, I will provide the nunnery with means to account for your stay with them, and you personally with enough gold to allow you to travel where you will. I would neither have you sell this, nor take it from you in compensation for my care of you."

With a nod of dismissal, Sir John left me and entered his office. I watched him go. As had happened the first time I'd come through the veil that separated my world from this one, I had found shelter, protection, and aid. How little I had known of the people of the past, even now with my advanced degrees in the subject, until I lived among them.

The next morning, I headed to the bailey where my escort of men and horses waited. I was to travel with a young girl, Elizabeth, and three of Sir John's men. Elizabeth had a vocation to be a nun, so Sir John was providing her the opportunity to pursue it. I didn't know their connection, but as in my case, it seemed he was paying for her out of the goodness of his heart.

I was apprehensive, having involved myself in a permanent lie that looked to stretch on for the foreseeable future—but was less worried than I'd been. I wasn't sorry to see the last of Sir John and Carlisle, especially if it meant getting me a little bit closer to Wales.

The travel consumed the morning and I forced myself to look around me, rather than dwell on my inner uncertainties. The Lake District of England is almost always lush and must have had a wet summer, because the streams were full and the grass was green. The country consisted of rolling hills, down to the little pocket of Armathwaite in which the nunnery nestled, at the junction of the rivers Coglin and Eden.

I followed the course of the Eden with my eyes. That river would lead me to the sea, and Wales, if only I could find a way to traverse that distance—a distance made all the greater because the only way to cross it was to go on foot, horseback, or by boat. Where was Marty and his plane? I felt bad at how lost he must feel and hoped he'd put the plane down further north, and found succor there.

The road widened as we came before the broad gates of the nunnery. The walls were comprised of a weathered, dark stone that I found welcoming instead of ominous. Sir John had told me that the nunnery was founded shortly after the Norman conquest in 1066. While technically within the jurisdiction of the Diocese of Carlisle, it treasured its isolation and independence. Apparently, the prioress was newly elected, but Sir John had heard good things of her. I was sure that Sir John was delighted to dump me on her, feeling his duty to me now done.

And so it turned out. We were greeted with courtesy. Women whisked Elizabeth off to the far reaches of the nunnery. An elderly nun showed me to a small cell with a pallet on the floor and a washbasin stand against one wall. A small window (no glass, but a shutter) overlooked the gardens. As the door shut behind her, I found myself releasing a breath I hadn't known I was holding. For as long as it took to find passage to Wales, I felt I could be safe here.

The nun said that I was free to wander the grounds that afternoon, which I did after washing my face and hands. I spent several hours exploring the gardens and the pretty walk along the river. At the bell, I returned, hoping for dinner, but a prayer service was held before the meal. I found a place at the back of the church. After the service, a nun led me to the private rooms of the prioress, where she said I would dine.

When I walked into the room, the prioress stood and we contemplated each other for a minute before I remembered myself and bobbed a curtsy. She bowed her head regally and indicated that I should sit in a chair on the other side of her desk.

"Good evening, Reverend Mother," I said, taking the offered chair. "I am most grateful to you for taking me in."

The woman tilted her head and gave a slight smile.

"You may call me 'Prioress Edyth', if you will," she said. "Sir John was most gracious in his request, and generous in his allowance." She waited for me to settle myself in front of what looked like an excellent roast mutton before she continued. "I was made to understand that you are a widow, with children. You seem quite young to have had so much befall you."

"Prioress," I said. "I would not like to continue with you the same misunderstanding I had with Sir John. I must tell you that I am thirty-seven years old, and my children are much grown."

She narrowed her eyes at me. "You do not look it. Many women would pay a great deal of money for your beauty secrets. Fortunately, we don't have such desires here. You will be quite safe."

Was she mocking me? Surely she was, but I couldn't tell from her serene expression. I swallowed hard. The turnip I'd just eaten stuck in my throat.

"I have heard something of how you came to be among us from Sir John's letter," Edyth said. "Is there anything you would like to add?"

"I do not know, Prioress Edyth, for I haven't read Sir John's letter," I said.

Edyth looked at me sharply. "So you read?" She tilted her head again. "You could be of benefit to our priory, but I understand that you desire to travel to Shrewsbury? May I ask your purpose, for Sir John has not related it here. He says that you are originally from Wales, from the royal court, even."

Instead of rendering her words entirely in English, the prioress used the Welsh word for Wales: 'Cymry.'

She gazed steadily at me with slate-gray eyes and a calm face. I guessed that she was about my own age—my real age. I found myself facing, for the first time, a woman from the thirteenth century with whom I sensed an actual connection. She was also quite strikingly beautiful. I couldn't see her hair, but thought it might be dark, like her brows and lashes, and I imagined that if she were dressed as I was, she could have married well above her rank.

I decided to take a risk. "My name is Marged," I said, replying to her in Welsh. "I am recently widowed and I hope to return home to my children, who are staying with my grandfather's family in Gwynedd. It is to Wales that I would like to travel."

Although she froze at my initial words, Edyth relaxed into her chair before I finished my sentence.

"I see," she said, also in Welsh. "Sir John knew of your connection to Gwynedd?"

"Yes, Prioress," I said. "Perhaps that is why he sent me to you? Can you help me to return home?"

She looked down at her desk and tapped one finger rhythmically on the edge. "It may be possible to help you," she said, after some thought. "I will ask my half-brother if he knows of a merchant who is traveling to Wales soon. Marc ... has some contacts."

She inspected me some more. "However, I would at least like the truth from you. Have you fled a convent? A second marriage you did not want? Did your father give you to an Englishman who has displeased you? Will I find a company of armed men on my doorstep in the morning, demanding your return?"

I looked at her, confused. "Pardon?"

"You might have fooled Sir John, but you cannot fool me so easily." The prioress waved a hand toward me. "You may be from the line of Ednyfed Fychan, but according to what you told Sir John, you haven't lived as well as that for many years. And yet, there is nothing about you that indicates a lowly existence in Shrewsbury. Your skin, your carriage, your ease of speech, your education, even your hands, belie your words!"

I looked down at my hands, now clenched together in my lap. They were soft as she said, not work-roughened, and I had trimmed my nails (though without polishing them, thankfully) the morning I boarded Marty's plane.

I looked up at her. "I don't know what to say."

Edyth was angry. I was angry too—at myself. I thought my story was pretty good considering the difficulties with my situation. Sir John had bought it, but Edyth was smarter than Sir John and I shouldn't have been surprised that it was easier to fool a man than another woman. I hated having to fool anyone. A long silence stretched between us.

"Fine," I said. "As a young woman, I was consort to Prince Llywelyn, the Prince of Wales, and bore him a son."

Edyth surged to her feet.

"You insult me with your stories and your lies!" She put her hands on her hips and glared at me. "What do you know of Prince Llywelyn's family? I am one of his casualties, and yet I will not allow you to impugn his name."

My chin had come up in response to her anger and my own outrage evaporated in the face of her defiance. "What did you say? How is it that you know Prince Llywelyn?"

Edyth scoffed under her breath. "I have never met the man, but my father, Evan, fought for him when he recaptured Cefnllys castle, many years ago. Unfortunately, in doing so, Prince Llywelyn aroused the anger of Roger Mortimer. To punish the Prince, Mortimer retaliated against the Welsh who lived within sight of his walls. We were evicted from our home."

"I'm sorry," I said, following her story without understanding its point.

Edyth shrugged. "I was only fifteen at the time. It was December, and my mother was carrying a child, though she wasn't so far along that one might notice. She and I struggled west, into Wales, but when she miscarried on the road, I couldn't do enough for her. Both she and the child died. When a sister to Prince Llywelyn heard of our fate, she offered to find a place for me in her own household. I was angry and defiant, however, and told my father that I wanted nothing of Wales, men, or marriage. I sought refuge in a place as far from home as possible. Eventually I found this nunnery, and my father brought me here."

She stepped around her desk and leaned down, her finger in my face.

"Now *that* is a story. Yours is pathetic in comparison. I will find you passage to Wales if only to be rid of you, but in the meantime, trouble me no more with your paltry explanations for I do not want to hear them."

Edyth passed me by and sailed from the room. The door slammed behind her.

Wow. I looked down at my hands. *I have never been very good at lying.*

* * * * *

The next morning, I saw Prioress Edyth in passing, and in church, but she didn't summon me and I tried to achieve patience. It wasn't as if I had a lot of free time. Bright and early, I found the nun hospitalier at my door, asking which service to the nunnery I would like to perform: weeding the garden, baking, or laundry. At first I was shocked by her request, but I assumed Edyth had ordered this, wanting me to get my hands dirty. I opted for the garden and the nun sent me to the herbalist who found a worn habit for me to wear and put me to work. I spent the day between the rows of plants.

It was enjoyable to garden in the summer sun, and I began to feel almost grateful to Edyth for giving me something to do. I was useful and satisfied—that is, until I woke up the next morning so stiff and sore I could barely move. I managed to haul myself out of bed anyway, and back onto my hands and knees.

After three more days of this, I was sent to the laundry. This was a job worth hating. The clothes were heavy and the water icy cold, even in August. Just as I thought I couldn't take any more, I was sent to the bakery. After three days kneading dough, it dawned on me that there was more to this than punishment for lying. Nearly two weeks had passed since my dinner with the Prioress, with no word from her, and it occurred to me that this must be some kind of test.

With that thought in mind, I waylaid her, as politely as I could, after services that evening.

"Prioress Edyth." I curtseyed. "Might I have a moment of your time?"

She stopped, stifled a sigh, and turned to me. "Are you finding your days with us worthwhile, Mistress Margaret? We do not work you too hard?"

"Madam." I was making an effort to disguise my impatience, but it was pretty feeble and I undoubtedly failed completely. "I was hoping that you have had word from your half-brother regarding my passage to Wales?"

"Come to me after dinner," Edyth said, instead of answering my question. "I can see that you have not found the contentment here I hoped for and you intend to continue with your previously stated course of action. We have enjoyed your good bread."

She swept away, leaving me thunderstruck. I couldn't believe it. *Good bread, indeed.*

In truth, it was my pride that was most hurt. I had believed, in the first hours of my walk along Hadrian's Wall, that I could control my destiny. Yes, I was a woman, but I was educated and intelligent, and had struggled and survived on my own with two children in the twenty-first century. Surely this counted for something? Surely what I'd learned in the last sixteen years and who I was now would make a difference? I was appalled to realize, several weeks later, that it had made no difference at all.

To Sir John, I'd been a burden. While grateful to me for helping his nephew, he had no use for me afterwards, no employment. I was a woman and a young and foolish one at that. Prioress Edyth knew of my intellectual abilities and believed that I'd grown up among the elite, but did she send me to the scriptorium or use my talents in any way? No, she put me to work in the kitchen.

Not that I minded baking or gardening, but in this world, women who could read were incredibly rare. And yet, two people who knew I had the skill had no use for me at all. On one hand, I was pleased that I could 'pass' as a medieval woman, but the truth was, I did not want to *be* a medieval woman. I never had and I found it frustrating and humiliating to be dependent on the kindness of others when I had skills I could offer them that would allow me to pay my own way.

Silently seething, I ate my meal as usual and then hurried to Edyth's study. I walked in to find her seated as before behind her desk, but this time she wasn't alone. She was having a discussion with a dark-haired man sitting with his right hip propped on her desk. He turned to look at me as I entered. His jaw dropped.

I froze.

I didn't recognize him, but because his expression was one of shock. It told me that he recognized *me*. Something about his face niggled at the back of my mind—and yet, how could I know him?

"You have met before?" Edyth said sharply.

The man's face cleared. "No, dear sister. I am just surprised she is so young. You said she was a widow."

Edyth's eyes narrowed, disbelief plain on her face, but at his impassivity, she turned to me. I managed to compose my face in an expression of innocence.

"I am ready to leave as soon as possible," I said.

Edyth pursed her lips but nodded. "Mistress Marged, this is my half-brother, Marc. Marc, this is Marged ferch—I am sorry, I don't remember your father's name."

"Bran," I said. *Why do I feel like everything she says to me is some kind of test?*

"Yes, Marged ferch Bran."

I curtsied and Marc bowed as we greeted each other.

"Now." Edyth rubbed her hands together. It seemed she'd decided to put the last few weeks behind her and was pleased to be ridding herself of me at last. "We must get Mistress Marged to Wales. I believe you said that you had some idea how this might be accomplished, Brother? I will give her a letter of introduction to St. Winifred's nunnery in

Conwy. They will take her in until she can make her way to her family."

"Yes, Sister," Marc said. "I can arrange it all if Mistress Marged can pay."

I got the feeling that his 'sister' was not as respectful as it could have been. I didn't see how I could go anywhere with this man, leastwise not until I figured out why he knew me.

Edyth glanced at me, and I nodded. Sir John had given me a few coins, as he'd promised. "She can pay, Marc. What do you have in mind?"

"Cousin Morgan is making a run to Anglesey," Marc said. "I have asked him to take her as passenger. He said he will do it, if the money is right." He turned to me. "The crossing is dangerous. The Irish Sea can be rough this time of year and the English haven't taken kindly to Prince Llywelyn's dominance of the region. They are harassing all ships that attempt to cross from England to Wales."

"Is there no other way for me to get there?" I said. Under the best of conditions, I was a poor sailor. I preferred the mountains of Wales to its seas.

"You could wait for a merchant train that travels south by land," Marc said. "However, Chester is an English stronghold and the Marcher lords guard the roads into

Wales. The journey would be nearly impossible for a woman alone."

I sighed inwardly. According to what little the nuns at the convent knew about current events—and I felt I could ask—Llywelyn's forces had won a great victory against King Edward in January of 1283. An unofficial truce now held between England and Wales, which is why I had to make my way to Wales by boat. "With no other real choice, I am willing to risk a sea crossing. How long is the journey?"

"You will sail west from Silloth on the coast, towards Ireland. Captain Morgan has an arrangement with the villagers that allows him to dock there unmolested. He intends to sail from there to the Isle of Man and come into Anglesey from the north and west. It is a journey of some days." Marc paused, and then said, "or, if the weather doesn't hold, you might not arrive at all."

I definitely didn't like Marc.

"It is slightly more than a league from here to Silloth," he said. "We will leave in two day's time. Once you arrive, he will want to sail on the evening tide."

"You will ensure that she reaches the boat safely, brother?" Edyth said.

"I will see to it personally, Sister." Marc smiled and bowed over Edyth's hand. As he did so, he glanced at me, and the expression on his face belied his jovial words. I took an involuntary step backwards and wondered desperately how I could avoid going anywhere with Marc.

"Very good, then," Edyth said. "Mistress Marged, if you could see Marc out, I would be most obliged."

"Certainly, Prioress." I made a curtsy and then opened the door to the office. Striving to keep well ahead of Marc, I led the way down the passage to the courtyard of the priory.

Although I walked quickly, the thudding of Marc's boots on the stones soon overtook my lighter steps. Just as I reached the doorway outside, he caught my arm. He pulled me back and crowded me against the doorpost.

"What are you doing here?" Marc hissed through gritted teeth. "You're supposed to be dead!"

"Am I?" I spit the words back at him because in that instant, I remembered who he was: one of the men that Prince Dafydd, Llywelyn's brother, kept around him. It had been Marc who had stood at his lord's side and grinned at me when Dafydd had 'rescued' me from the river near Castell y Bere. I could appreciate his surprise at seeing me again, but I didn't understand his anger.

"Do you think to return to Prince Llywelyn, is that it?" Marc said.

"Yes." I glared at Marc, defiant.

"I should kill you where you stand. It is *your* fault that I no longer serve Prince Dafydd. *Your* fault that he dispensed with my services."

"My fault? How could that be *my* fault? I haven't been to Wales in sixteen years!"

"You—" Marc cut off his words, apparently so angry he couldn't reply. His jaw bulged. "I will escort you to the sea, simply to see you on your way so you may never trouble me again."

"How do I know you will do as you say? I can't trust you." My words were probably unwise, but I needed to know his full intentions.

Marc caught my chin in his hand and tipped it up so the back of my head clonked into the wall and my ears rang.

"You try my patience, woman! Be glad my sister has put her hand over you and keep your tongue between your teeth!"

With that he released me and stalked off. I watched him go, rubbing the back of my head, and thinking that perhaps that was the best advice I had been given in some time.

5

Two days later, Marc came for me at dawn, as he had promised. I wondered at the propriety of our journeying together, even if only for a day. Perhaps, because I was a widow, I was allowed this kind of freedom. It could also have been that Prioress Edyth was happy to get me off her hands in any fashion she could. Sort of like Sir John, in point of fact. *I guess at thirty-seven, I am a far less endearing person than I was at twenty.*

I debated returning to Prioress Edyth and trying again to convince her that I knew Marc from when I'd lived with Llywelyn, but in the end decided against it. By now, I didn't have very many choices—*did I have any choices?*—and although I didn't trust Marc, he appeared to have a certain sort of honor. To make myself feel safer, I stole a small knife from the kitchen and secreted it in my pack. If Marc was determined to kill me, it wouldn't be of much use, but it helped me keep a grip on rationality.

It was a fine day in late August—perfect for jogging along on the horse Marc had provided. For over an hour after we left the convent, Marc didn't say a single word to me. He rode a few yards ahead, his shoulders stiff and his back straight. Clearly, our meeting had brought up bad memories and he hadn't forgiven me for whatever it was that he believed I'd done.

And truly, I wanted to know what that was. "When did you leave Prince Dafydd's service?" I raised my voice so my words could cross the yards that separated us.

I thought at first that he wasn't going to answer, he took so long to speak, but then he said, "Earlier this year."

"How, then, can your leaving him be my fault?"

But Marc had gone mute again. As a result, I dropped further behind him. In the weeks since I'd arrived, I'd thought of little else but that single year with Llywelyn that had changed my life so completely. Marc had barely played into it, which is why it had taken so long to recognize him— that and the years hadn't been as kind to him as they'd apparently been to me. He'd been there at the river. I'd seen him in the company of Prince Dafydd during his visit to Brecon when I was pregnant with David. What had Marc done to turn Prince Dafydd against him sixteen years later that had anything to do with me?

Suddenly, two men on horseback burst from the woods in front of Marc. One of them held a sword. I reined in, my horse feeling my panic and skittering sideways.

"Stay away from me!" Fifty feet ahead of me, Marc's horse danced away from the two others.

I didn't know what to do. I sidled my horse to the side of the road, warring between turning tail and running and staying to help—if I even could. It wasn't as if I could ride to Marc's rescue.

The man with the sword had fair hair and a short, stocky build. He stuck out his chin at Marc. "You dare to give me orders?"

Marc, however, wasn't intimidated. "Is this not cowardly, Henry?" He pulled out his sword too and waved it at the lead rider. "Are your orders to dispose of me now? Why can't Prince Dafydd let me live in peace?"

"You failed in your duty, Marc." Henry's voice was all reason, as if it was perfectly acceptable for him to attack Marc in the middle of the day and Marc should simply yield. "You know too much about his plans. The Prince lives, and thus, you must die."

My brain could barely process Henry's words. Prince Dafydd had plotted against Llywelyn *again*? Is that what they were talking about?

For all that Llywelyn had tried to protect me from scenes such as this, I had seen violence when I'd lived with him. But I hadn't faced a sword in so long, the fear caught me by surprise, closing my throat and making my heart beat in my ears. I felt disembodied, hovering above the men as they hacked at each other and as the historian in me objectively observed how awkward it was to try to fight on horseback.

Although he received at least one solid blow to the head from the unnamed second man's shield, Marc was able to ram his sword through the man's stomach before slashing the throat of Henry's horse. Henry slipped his feet from the stirrups before the horse could crush him and landed on his feet. From the saddle, Marc swung his sword at him. Henry backed way and balanced on the edge of the road, in danger of losing his footing on the soft ground near the trees.

Marc, in this incarnation, had no regrets or recriminations. He face had fallen into grim and determined lines. He wasn't going to lie down and die before Henry.

"You betrayed us, Marc!" Henry voice carried above the trees. "It is by your cowardice that the Prince still lives. If you have any loyalty left towards Prince Dafydd, you will put up your sword and come with me now."

"And allow you to murder me the moment I lower my guard?" Cursing his denial, Marc struck Henry's sword such a blow that Henry dropped it. Marc leaned forward, grabbed Henry by the upper arm and jerked him so that he was standing on his tiptoes. "You dare come at me with your accusations?" Marc said. "You know nothing about me or what I have done."

"Prince Dafydd—"

"Prince Dafydd let me go. I don't care if you tell him that you found me. He will know you failed to subdue me. The next time I see you, I *will* kill you."

I believed Marc, and Henry took him at his word too. Marc loosened his grip and Henry twisted away. Five seconds later, he had leaped the ditch beside the road and disappeared into the trees that lined it. Marc let him go, and then like the felling of a great tree in the forest, tilted sideways in the saddle, slid off his horse, and landed with a hollow thump on the ground.

I dismounted and ran forward to fall on my knees at Marc's side. Truth be told, even if Marc hated me, I needed him. If he died I didn't know what I would do. Perhaps I could journey to the ship by myself for the short distance remaining, but I feared encountering Henry or other strange men. It wasn't like I was dressed as a nun.

I patted Marc's body up and down but the only blood on him was spray from the man he'd killed. The blow to his head must have been worse than it first appeared, and I was glad that Marc hadn't keeled over until after Henry had gone.

"I should have known better than to major in history." I mumbled the words to myself as I eased Marc's helmet from his head. "Nursing would have served me better."

The blow to Marc's head had dented his helmet and produced an ugly knot where Henry had struck him. A sliver of metal was embedded in his skin and blood seeped from the wound, clotting in his hair.

For a moment, I wished I still had my pocket-sized first aid kit, but then dismissed the thought. I couldn't doctor Marc properly, but I wasn't entirely without resources.

When I'd come to the nunnery, I'd possessed nothing other than what I stood up in. But Prioress Edyth had given me a parting gift of a satchel with a change of clothes, food, and a water skin, plus a medieval version of a first aid kit: a salve of sanicle, tweezers, and some linen bandages. She must have known her brother better than I'd thought.

With the metal tweezers, which looked remarkably like ones I might have purchased from a store at home, I drew the sliver out. It wasn't long, but it had been stopping up the wound, which now bled freely.

Hurrying now lest Marc lose too much blood, I pressed a cloth against the wound. The blood had soaked his hair, but I cleared the area around the wound and sponged at it gently with a second damp cloth. It was just as well, in truth, that I didn't have my original first aid kit. Marc probably would woken up, balked at the packaging, and decided I was a witch, on top of my other failings.

Part of me would have preferred to leave him in the dust and continue the journey by myself, but I couldn't do it. Just because he hated me, didn't mean I could abandon him in his distress. It was some comfort that at this point he needed me more than I needed him.

Pressing firmly, I eventually stemmed the bleeding, and then wrapped his head with a strip of linen. Even after I finished, I stayed on the ground, cradling his head in my lap and waiting for him to wake.

He didn't stir. I sat there, feeling more and more uncomfortable in my exposed position and trying to figure out what I would do if he never woke. I had two horses, a road the end of which I didn't know, and an unconscious man whom I couldn't hope to lift onto a horse. I wasn't too happy about the dead man and a couple of feet from me either.

I was starting to wonder if I really should leave Marc, in order to seek help in a nearby village (provided I could find one) when Marc moaned and jerked his shoulders. He tried to sit up, but fell back, his hand to his head. No doubt he found his position on my lap as uncomfortable as I did, because he grimaced at me and tried to put me in my place.

"What have you done to me, woman?" he said. "My head aches like the devil himself were inside it!"

"You received a blow to the head and fell off your horse," I said. "You bled everywhere, but I bound your wound and hopefully, if you go slowly, your wound will heal."

He glared at me, but I returned his gaze without animosity. He grumbled to himself and very slowly sat up. I scooted away and handed him the water skin so he could drink. After a few more minutes, he was able to lever himself to his feet. He rested his head against his horse and slowly stroked its neck.

"Are we in danger from Henry, do you think?" I said.

Marc sighed and patted his horse some more, back to his usual silence. Fortunately, this time, he condescended to break it. "Henry is my cousin," he said in a level voice, the first time I'd heard him use it. "While Edyth and I share a father, Henry is the eldest son of my father's brother. Upon his deathbed, my uncle asked me to look after him. Henry is five years younger than I, and has always been greedy, conniving, and very, very intelligent. I thought I could control him, and failed in the worst possible way.

"Since Prince Dafydd returned to Wales—after the agreement of 1277—Henry rose higher in the Prince's estimation, to my detriment. It was through me that Henry came to the Prince's attention in the first place, but I realize now that Henry continually whispered untruths about me in the Prince's ear. Prince Dafydd, in turn, saw the possibilities in my brother: that he would carry out his bidding, no matter what it was. That brought Henry more power. Through Henry's urging, Prince Dafydd reconciled with Prince Llywelyn. As Prince Dafydd's influence grew, so did Henry's."

"What plan did you fail to complete that brought down Prince Dafydd's ire on you?" I said. "Did he order you to ... assassinate Prince Llywelyn?"

Marc opened one eye and then closed it, before answering a question I hadn't asked. "Henry rescued me from my debtors, but I owed him money and he never let me forget it. He threatened to expose my failings to my other creditors. And to Prince Dafydd, if I didn't take the blame for something I didn't do. That the plan failed is Henry's doing, not mine."

"What plan?"

But Marc didn't answer. He gripped his horse's mane and pulled himself into the saddle as if he were climbing the last peak of a tall mountain range. Once in the saddle, he looked first at me, and then away down the road.

"I will speak no more of this," he said. "It is over. Now remount your horse and we will be on our way."

He urged his horse forward and I hurried to catch my own horse and mount, my head spinning all the while. The need to see Llywelyn had risen as an ache in my breast I hadn't felt for many years. I'd fought it; I'd beaten it down; I'd suppressed it to the point that I believed I could live a normal life. I *had* lived a normal life. But all I'd done was lull myself into living a lie.

For the rest of the day, I rode well behind Marc. Whether his silence was due to shame or anger I did not know. I was as lost in the Middle Ages as I'd ever been.

* * * * *

"You must be Mistress Marged," the stocky captain of the *Morgannwg* said in Welsh as I dismounted. Marc was already turning his horse around as if he meant to leave that very minute.

"Yes, sir," I said in the same language, glancing back at Marc. "How soon do we sail?"

"With the tide, Madam. One hour. Please come aboard."

I glanced past him to the little boat that would carry me to Wales and thought ugly thoughts.

"Are there any other passengers?" I wanted to know how many others might witness my upcoming humiliation.

The captain hesitated, leaned forward, and lowered his voice. "There is one, Madam. He should remain hidden and you need not encounter him."

"Why ever not?"

"He is a physician." Morgan pursed his lips, thinking. "He is ... a Jew."

"Oh," I said.

"The man saved my daughter's life and I feel I must accommodate his request for passage to Wales. If you are concerned about sailing with him ..."

The man hesitated again and I hurried to reassure him. "I'm not concerned, sir. Please don't worry about him on my account. I confess I am not a good sailor, and I might have need of his assistance on the voyage."

The captain opened his mouth as if to speak, seemed to think better of it, and then blurted out his thoughts anyway. "But, Madam! The Archbishop of Canterbury has forbidden Jewish physicians to practice on English Christians."

The light dawned. I had momentarily forgotten about this odious era of English history.

"Then it's a good thing we're not English, isn't it?" I swept up the gangplank past him.

"It is, indeed, Madam." The captain barked a laugh behind me. "It is indeed."

I found myself on board a single-masted, single-ruddered, cargo vessel that was larger than I had initially thought. Did I want to know what goods he was hauling illegally to Wales? *Probably not.* It could be food, since drugs were an unlikely source of illicit income in the thirteenth century. The hatch on the main deck was open, revealing a dark space below decks. Two low-ceilinged cabins sat on the deck at the rear of the boat, one for me and one for the captain. Where was the physician staying? *Please not in the cargo hold!*

I turned around, just as one of the sailors put my satchel on board the ship. Morgan stood at Marc's stirrup.

He hadn't actually left yet. Marc nodded at something Morgan said and then looked at me.

I raised my hand. "Thank you, Marc."

He hesitated, and then returned my salutation, before grasping the reins of both his horse and mine and heading back the way we'd come. Meanwhile, a different sailor picked up my satchel, opened the cabin door, and gestured that I should follow him inside.

"Where should I put this, Madam?" he said, in Welsh.

"In the corner is fine," I said.

He dropped it on the floor and left. I surveyed the space that would be my living quarters for the next few days. The furniture included a single chair and table, which was bolted to the floor, and a cloth sling hanging from the ceiling in one corner. It was a hammock, though the captain wouldn't have used the word and I hadn't thought they were known in Europe before the Spanish Conquest. It made me scoff yet again at all historians didn't get quite right.

I exited my cabin to find the captain just closing the door of the cabin beside mine. Glancing at me, he pulled it shut, but not before I saw the figure of a man, sitting at a table in the far corner. *The physician.* I was relieved not to have to think the worst of Captain Morgan.

"We sail within the hour, Madam," the Captain said.

"Thank you." I followed him up the ladder to the top deck. He indicated that I could sit under the canopy at the rear of the boat. I did as he suggested and watched the sun set. It wasn't clear to me how, exactly, the captain was going to navigate us to Wales in the dark. The thirteenth century might not be pre-hammock, but we were definitely pre-sextant.

The Isle of Man was some distance south and west of Silloth, the village at which we were docked. I couldn't see the island from where I sat. Hopefully, Captain Morgan had an astrolabe, and between that and dead reckoning, he could find the way.

This proved to be the case, at least for the initial stage of our journey. It took us all night to sail to the Isle of Man, and all of the next day to reach Keill Moirrey, a fishing village on the south end of the island. Because Scotland, not England, ruled the Isle of Man in this time, the village could offer us a safe haven.

Unfortunately, smooth sailing or not, within an hour of leaving Silloth and entering the Irish Sea, I was hanging over the side of the boat, praying for the journey to end. The crew managed to refrain from openly laughing at me, but I could see laughter in their eyes—when I could open mine, that is. As a teenager, I had once gone deep sea fishing with my aunt and uncle. I'd caught a tuna in that first hour of relative peace, and spent the remaining eight hours on the boat lying on a cushion feeling ill. I'd avoided small boats—any boat, really—ever since. The memory hadn't improved with time, and this journey felt (if possible) worse.

I was so miserable that I didn't remember to ask for help from the physician until after we left Keill Moirrey. It was the captain's comment, "Rough sea ahead!" that reminded me. I leapt to my feet and knocked on the door of the other cabin.

"Come in." The words were in English.

I opened the door and stepped through it, finding myself in a space equal in size to mine, with its own hammock and table. An older man with a beard and long gown sat in a chair near the starboard window. He got to his feet as I entered, and greeted me with a bow. I curtsied, which seemed to surprise him, and he suggested I sit in the only other chair in the room.

I sat and for a minute we just looked at each other.

He spoke first, again in English. "I am Aaron ben Simon." Then, with a wry smile, he added, "I confess you are not what I expected."

I'd heard that a lot recently. "How is that?" I said.

"The captain led me to believe that you were a widow with two grown children. I had envisioned a woman with more years to her. You are young and beautiful."

If I were on the internet, I would have typed *LOL*. That was one of the nicest things anyone had said to me in a long time. I should have been used to everyone's reaction to my appearance by now, but I kept forgetting. Life was hard for women in the Middle Ages, even those who were rich. By comparison, the twenty-first century provided a very soft life, and that was reflected in my face, and as Edyth had noticed, my hands.

I smiled and thanked him. "My name is Meg, and I assure you that I am long widowed. I am thirty-seven years old, though few have believed this of me of late."

Aaron's eyes smiled, even if his mouth didn't. "How is it that you were in England?"

All of a sudden, I realized he was the first person I had met here who was really looking at *me* and talking to *me*; not to a preconception of me that included woman, widow, and dependent person. It made me wonder who Aaron was and if he was representative of the Jewish community in England. I knew he was probably well educated; certainly he was literate if he was a doctor.

I had a sudden compulsion to tell him the truth—the real truth—but I clamped my lips together and fought the feeling. He watched me, and I decided that some truth was better than none.

"Please forgive me my silence," I said. "I would rather not lie to you, and that means I can't tell you anything of myself. Will you accept me as I am for the time being? Hopefully, when we arrive in Wales, I can tell you more of my history."

Aaron graciously tipped his head. I sighed in relief.

"I was hoping that you could help me with my seasickness," I said. "I understand that you are a doctor?"

"Yes." His expression grew concerned. "But I am forbidden to practice on Christians."

"English Christians," I reminded him, "which I am most definitely not. We are also no longer under the jurisdiction of England, so perhaps you would consider helping me?"

"I would be delighted to assist you." Aaron rose to his feet. "If you give me a moment, I will find something that should stem your nausea."

"Thank you." I watched as he went to a trunk, pulled out a large book, and began to page through it.

"What is that book?" I said, after a minute.

"A Greek text," Aaron said, without turning around. "Why do you ask?"

"That's too bad. I can't read Greek."

Aaron almost dropped the book. "You read, Madam? In what language?"

"In English, Welsh, French, and Spanish," I said. "And Latin."

Aaron stared at me, and I couldn't help feeling pleased. *Finally,* someone who appreciated my particular talents. Young and beautiful was all very well and good—but smart was better. It hadn't always been that way for me, which is probably why I'd allowed myself to fall for Anna's father, but I wasn't eighteen anymore.

Aaron didn't question me further, however, because a second later a loud rushing sound came from outside. In unison, we looked towards the doorway, which I had left open for propriety's sake. Rain beat on the deck so hard I could barely see the wood through the rush of water. The boat had been rolling more and more as Aaron and I had been talking, but our conversation had distracted me from the rocky feeling in my stomach. Now my attention was drawn to it, and the intense queasiness returned. I must have paled because Aaron hurried to his herbal collection and began taking down bottles.

"I cannot promise the immediacy of the cure," he said, stirring one powder and then another into a glass of wine. "By rights you should have taken this before we left land, for it to reach full potency by the time we reached the open sea."

"Anything to help me." I gurgled my unhappiness, my head in my hands. Aaron handed me the wine.

I gazed at it, not dubiously, but suddenly wary of medieval medicine I didn't know anything about. "What's in it?"

"Ginger, basil, and peppermint are the best herbs for nausea. Their tastes don't go well together, however, and usually I use just one, infused in a tea. I have no hot water here and thus, I ground the herbs to powder and mixed them with wine. This particular concoction is predominantly ginger. I am out of peppermint."

Feeling like I had to drink it, if only so Aaron wouldn't think I mistrusted him, I sipped the drink. It didn't taste too bad—a good thing because that alone could have made me vomit. I sipped some more and thanked him as he returned to his chair.

"What brings you to this ship?" I said, trying to distract myself from my stomach. "Captain Morgan told me that you'd saved his daughter's life. Why are you leaving England?"

"I may have saved her life, but I lost my wife and daughter in the same sickness."

"I am so sorry!" I said. "How terrible for you!"

"Fortunately, Samuel, my son, was not with us and was spared."

The silence stretched out and I was about to prompt him again, when he spoke. "I have worried about the status of Jewry in England for many years. King Henry took our money and allowed us a living, such as it was, but his son, Edward, stripped us of our wealth and standing. He has even closed the synagogues. Many refuse to see the danger, but I am free to make my way in the world. If a more hospitable land exists, I will try to find it."

"And you think that might be Wales?" I said.

"Prince Llywelyn exhibits few of the excesses of his English cousins. He doesn't persecute the Jews, and he himself is under the interdict of excommunication. He ignores this by worshipping among the Cistercians, who have no love for the Jews, I admit, but their rule is more tolerant than that of their English brethren."

"I see," I said, loving the formality of his vocabulary, and thinking of all the people who left Europe for America over the centuries for the freedom to practice their religion in peace. That was still over three hundred years in the future. Aaron's decision to sail to Wales was only a first step.

Aaron tilted his head to one side as if curious. "For some reason, I believe you really do see. How is that possible?"

"It is one of things I can't tell you right now, without having to lie," I said. "And I am tired of lying."

Aaron nodded and then looked more closely at me. "Your face is turning green. " He said this if making an unimportant observation.

"I feel terrible."

"Let us walk a little," Aaron said. "Perhaps the captain would allow me on the deck to escort you to the side of the boat."

I nodded and Aaron took my arm. We walked through the door and then a few paces to the left, trying to stay in the shelter of the slight overhang that protected us from the rain. I gripped the rail, but then saw with horror how enormous the waves had become. As the boat went up one wave and down another it seemed that a gulf opened at our feet.

"Madam! Have a care! And you!" Captain Morgan appeared with a glare for Aaron. "What are you thinking?"

"Sorry! Sorry!" Aaron held up his hands, palms outward. "My mistake."

"Get yourselves back inside!" Captain Morgan grasped our arms and hauled us backwards from the rail and towards the cabin door. As the deck of the boat rose again, we fell into Aaron's cabin and the Captain slammed the door behind us.

I found myself face down, my dress rucked up around my thighs. Fortunately, since I'd been riding astride during my journey, I wore leggings underneath.

I pushed to my hands and knees. "I hate the sea."

"I can appreciate why," Aaron said.

Laughter bubbled in my throat and then bile. I forced it back down. Everything that had happened over the last week threatened to overwhelm me all at once and I moaned. Aaron hooked his hand around my arm and helped me into the hammock. I rocked with the motion of the ship, listening to the rain pound on the roof and praying that I—and this little boat—could keep it together just a little longer.

6

The storm worsened in the night. Aaron hung on to an iron ring in the floor, literally for dear life, while I rocked in the hammock. He tried to make conversation, but I felt so ill I could barely speak. He talked about his family, particularly of his older brother Jacob, who had been a trouble-maker as a boy. When I didn't respond, even to his funnier stories, he began to recite one of his medical books from memory. In Latin.

At some point in the dark hours of the early morning, Captain Morgan reappeared. As he opened the door, the wind banged it back against the wall of the room so hard that it split in two. "Mistress! You must leave the ship with the youngsters among my crew. We are only a few miles from Wales but I can't take the ship in to shore. The storm hasn't lessened as I'd hoped and the wind is against us."

Terror filled me, though there was something in Morgan's eyes that made me think he was offering us the only hope he had, and would save none for himself. Without waiting for an answer, he half-dragged, half-carried me from the room, picking up Aaron by his upper arm on his way out the door.

"We will launch the dinghy," Morgan said. "My crew will see you safe to Anglesey."

I didn't ask him what he was going to do, or if he honestly thought he would survive this. I'd lived in Wales for long enough—and been back in the Middle Ages for long enough—to understand that there were times when you didn't question a man's decision to face death head on.

"What about my books—?"

Aaron broke off his question at Morgan's disbelieving look.

"We will find other books, Aaron," I said. " As rare as yours may be, they are not the only ones. Your life, however, is the only one you have."

"Thank you, Madam," Morgan said. "I couldn't have said it better myself."

Aaron acquiesced without asking me why I was so confident I could acquire new books for him. That would mean I'd have to tell him about Llywelyn, and not only was I not ready to do that, it would expose my own insecurities: *What if Llywelyn didn't want to see me? What if this world he'd created had no room for me in it?*

We staggered across the deck, barely maintaining our feet on the rocking ship. The rain had soaked us instantly. Wave after wave crashed over the bow and we essentially fell over the rail of the ship when it was at its lowest point and into the dingy that rose up on the next wave to catch us. *God, I hate boats.* The four crewmen who would travel with us pushed away from the ship. I clung to Aaron's arm.

"We'll make it!" he said, but a moment later, the dingy met a driving wave exactly wrong and capsized, dumping us into the sea.

Amazingly, I bobbed up for air without my lungs full of water. "Aaron!" I spun around, searching for him, trying not to panic. Ideally, I hoped all survived the capsizing, but in the last hours, Aaron and I had become friends. I wanted him to be okay.

"I'm here." He appeared beside me, struggling out of his heavy robes. We had loosened the ties on our cloaks in the dingy, knowing that if we ended up in the water, they would drag us down. As I ripped off my cloak and shoved it away from me, an abandoned oar floated past. I grabbed it. The rain pounded so hard I could barely see Aaron through the water streaming down my face, much less anyone else, or our lost boat.

"We're not as far from shore as Morgan implied," Aaron said.

"How do you know? I can't see anything." But just then a wave lifted me up and I saw the shore. It wasn't close enough to touch, but it gave me hope.

"Can you swim?" Aaron said.

"Not well," I said, scissor-kicking my legs even as I spoke. It was true. But I *could* swim, and at this point, I had no other choice. With one hand each on the oar, and the other helping paddle, we stroked and kicked, each wave lifting us and surging us closer to shore. The tide was bringing us in.

"Wake up, Margaret!" Aaron's voice roused me. I hadn't realized I was floating and no longer swimming.

"Okay," I said, though he probably didn't know what that meant. I began to kick again.

* * * * *

When I woke up, the sun was shining brightly in my face. I lay still a moment, feeling the heat on my closed lids, and then opened them. As is often the case after a storm in Wales, the sky above me was a bright blue, with a few scattered clouds, and gave no sign of the horrors of a few hours before. Experimentally, I moved a leg and then my arms. Bruises? *Check.* Aching muscles? *Check.* Seemingly nothing was broken, however. I eased into a sitting position. It hurt to move so much I choked out a laugh. *I will never, ever set foot on a boat again.*

Around me, the beach was littered with refuse thrown up by the surf, mostly driftwood and seaweed, but here and there was a wine cask or the remains of a boat. But no Aaron.

With legs aching, I got to my feet. My clothes had dried in the sun but I could feel the salt and sand in my hair and a pass through it with my fingers told me it stuck up on end. I smoothed it the best I could. Llywelyn could be only a short walk away, if only I knew where I was.

And then I laughed at myself for my foolishness in thinking that Llywelyn would be anywhere near here, and that even if he were, he would want anything to do with me. I had left him and taken his child with me, even if unintentionally. That might not be something he could forgive.

I started walking down the beach, angling away from the water and towards the dunes in the distance. The morning sun shone bright in my eyes and I put up a hand to shade them. Some people had clustered on the edge of the beach and I peered towards them, hoping one was Aaron.

As I got closer, a man broke away and my heart leapt. It *was* Aaron. He was alive!

"Meg!" he said.

Aaron hiked up his robe and took off at a run towards me. I waved and veered towards him to meet him half-way between the dunes and the sea. Always wary of touching a gentile, Aaron ducked the hug I was about to throw at him and took my forearms decorously.

Then Aaron turned me towards two of his companions, who had followed him. The closer they came, the more my eyes watered. By the time they had taken ten steps, tears poured down my cheeks and blurred my vision.

"Oh, my God, it's Mom."

David stood before me, saying those words. *David!*

The sound of his voice released Anna and she raced across the beach towards me, her boots slipping in the sand. Sobbing, she threw herself into my arms and knocked me backwards. I held her, my cheek against her hair, rocking her as if she were a baby. She *was* my baby.

"Oh, my darling daughter." I repeated the words over and over again. If I said them enough, I could believe that she was in my arms. Anna couldn't stop crying, even when I took her face in my hands and kissed her eyes, trying to get her to stop.

"It's okay. It's me. I'm here." I looked past Anna to David, who'd come to a halt five paces away, as if he couldn't believe what he was seeing either. "And your brother too." I held out one arm and he came into the circle of it. I embraced both my children for the first time in a year and a half.

"How did you get here?" Anna said.

I shook my head. "It's a long story." David's shoulder muffled my voice. "I can't believe you're here, too. I didn't let myself believe it might be possible."

We hugged and rocked until the tightness in my chest loosened and I was able to relax my hold enough to look into my children's faces.

"You must have been through a lot," Anna said.

"Me?" I said, and laughed through my tears. "What about you? Have you been here all this time?"

"We have," David said. "Let's get you home." He put his arm around my shoulders and looked at Anna over the top of my head. *Over the top of my head!* When I'd last seen him, we'd been same height.

Anna held tight to my hand as David herded us, along with a very bemused Aaron, back to where they'd left their horses.

"You mentioned that you had known the Prince many years ago," Aaron said, "but I didn't quite catch that you'd given him a son."

"I couldn't tell you and I didn't want to lie," I said, and left it at that.

A few steps further on, a man waited—tall, dark, and handsome, with the deep blue eyes of a Celt. Anna took the man's hand and pulled him towards me. "This is my husband, Mom, Mathonwy ap Rhys Fychan."

"I'm pleased to meet you, Madam," Math said, his Welsh formal.

I stuck out my hand, as if meeting Anna's husband was a perfectly normal thing to do, but then ruined it. "You're married?" I blurted out the words before I could take them back. My hand went to my head before Math could shake it. "How can you be married?"

Anna tightened her grip on Math's other hand. "I'm sorry you missed it, Mom, but, well … you weren't here."

With that, I melted again. I started crying and then Anna started crying, and we fell into each other's arms. Math kissed the top of Anna's head and patted her on the shoulder.

"We'll leave you a moment." He and Aaron moved past us towards the horses and out of earshot.

Once again, Anna and I struggled to regain our composure, wiping at our cheeks with the backs of our hands.

"How long have you been back here?" The control in David's voice told me he was determined to remain on an even keel. *So like Llywelyn.*

"Since the beginning of August," I said. "I think."

"*How* did you get back here?" Anna said, finally able to calm down enough to marshal her thoughts.

"By plane," I said. "Near Hadrian's Wall."

"Hadrian's Wall?" David said. "And you made it here all by yourself?"

"I had help," I said, "most recently Aaron's."

"Hadrian's Wall is a long way from here," Anna said.

"It is," David said. "Father is going to freak."

7

I froze, my hand on David's shoulder, my face like a frozen mask. "Father?" I wasn't ready. I'd thought about him every waking moment since I came back to the Middle Ages, but I still wasn't ready.

"He's alive, Mom," David said. "And he's here, at Rhuddlan Castle."

"Oh, David." I put the back of my hand to my mouth. "I didn't dare ... I mean, I hardly dared to even think that he might be, that I might be able to see him again. So you think ..." I stopped.

"Do I think he'll want to see you?" David said. "Yeah, I know he will."

"But how did you ... how did you find him? How did you know he was your father?"

"I didn't," David said. "Father did though, the moment we arrived. We literally drove into his attackers at Cilmeri and saved him."

"He *went* to Cilmeri?!" I couldn't help it. My voice went high. "He *went* to Cilmeri on December 11th?"

"It's okay, Mom," Anna said, in a voice that said *patience*, and was probably one she'd heard from me a million times growing up. "He felt he had to, despite your warning."

"He could have died!" I glared at David and then at Anna, and then she and I burst into tears again.

I could feel David staring at us in amazement, thinking *they should be happy!*

I turned to my son, my cheeks wet, blinking my eyes to rid them of tears. "This is too much to take in. You were a child last time I saw you, David, and now you are grown and Anna is married." I turned back to Anna. "You got married at what—eighteen?"

"Math's a great guy, Mom," David said. "He can't believe how lucky he is to have her; and the marriage secures a beneficial alliance for Father. It's all worked out really well."

"Besides, I'm nineteen now," Anna said.

I stared at them for a second and then gave a laugh that was almost a bark. "See! Precisely my point!" And then, more thoughtfully, "Does Math know where you're from?"

Anna nodded. "He *knows*, but I think he's just beginning to *believe*."

"It's always been impossible to believe," I said. "And I'm living it."

"Math is pretty grounded in the here and now," David said. "He told me that if Anna looks Welsh, speaks Welsh, and is acknowledged as Welsh by the Prince of Wales, that is good enough for him."

"I guess there is something to be said for that," I said. "We will need hard-headed and practical people in the new Wales."

"Don't you remember when you came to Wales the first time?" Anna said. "Do you remember what it was like trying to find your way when you didn't speak the language and knew nothing about anything that was important?"

I sighed. "I do remember. I remember very well. If not for Llywelyn, I don't know that I would have survived. Before I knew it, we were in love and I was pregnant with David. I managed to bypass most of the trauma by ignoring it."

"We couldn't ignore it, Mom," Anna said. "It was all so awful at first."

I nodded. "I know, sweetheart. That you're standing in front of me, whole and happy, tells me that you and David have done remarkably well, at a much younger age than I was."

"We did have each other," Anna said.

"And we also had Father who knew who we were from the start," David said.

"It would have been different if we'd appeared in Cilmeri and *not* killed Papa's attackers," said Anna. "Imagine trying to make your way in Wales with no help from anyone. We could have starved to death. David could have ended up a stable boy, and me a scullery maid."

"Or worse." My expression darkened.

"A lot worse!" Anna said. "Imagine if the English had captured us!"

More settled, at least for the moment, we walked back to the horses. David mounted his horse and pulled me up behind him. "So, how did you get from Hadrian's Wall to Wales?" David turned the horse's head and headed south, towards Rhuddlan. "Planes, trains, automobiles?"

"Try feet and horses," I said. "And then, of course, the ship."

"I'm sorry, Mom." David said. "How bad was the seasickness?"

"That's how I made friends with Aaron," I said. "He gave me a concoction to settle my stomach, which helped, and then he kept me distracted from my stomach by stories of his family. In the end, though, it didn't make any difference since the storm broke up the boat and dumped us into the sea."

Within half an hour, we approached the castle. Every yard made me feel more sick to my stomach than I'd been on the boat. As we rode under the gatehouse, I glanced up to see a familiar figure standing at the top of one of the towers. Llywelyn looked down at me—and it felt like the whole world paused and took a breath.

"It's Llywelyn." I gripped the back of David's cloak. "I look terrible! My hair, my clothes are full of salt. I don't even have shoes. He can't see me like this."

David ignored me, not dignifying my concerns with a response. Llywelyn left the battlements and reappeared at ground level. He crossed the bailey with his characteristic long stride, his head steady and his eyes fixed on me, and then halted at my knee. He reached for me. My heart breaking and healing in the same instant, I slid into his arms.

"I never meant to leave you, Llywelyn. I didn't want to keep your son from you."

Llywelyn slipped one arm around my waist and brought me close to him while threading his other hand through my hair. "I never for a moment thought you did," he said. And kissed me.

* * * * *

Later that evening, after all the hubbub had died down and Llywelyn and I were alone, I sat on a stool by his chair in front of the fire, resting my head against his knee. We'd sat this way so many times when I was pregnant with David, it felt like I'd fallen through time—not just to Wales— but to when I was a girl.

But I wasn't that girl—or even *a* girl—and the world was a different place now. Not just my world either, but his too. Neither of us were the same people who'd parted sixteen years ago, and that would take some getting used to.

Llywelyn rested his hand on my hair. He'd kissed me long and hard, not just the once but many times. He was determined, however, to abide by the Church's restrictions for as long as it took to organize our wedding. In our hearts, we'd been married all along—and even been married legally if Llywelyn had been a commoner. All it took to be married in Wales in the Middle Ages was for both parties to claim it and consummate it. But to say so would have nullified his marriage to Elinor (who had died in 1282 giving birth to his daughter). Neither of us wanted to do that.

"Something is troubling you," he said. I looked up at him, noting his serious tone. He smiled down at me. "More than you might be troubled by this change in your fortunes for a second time."

"I don't quite know where to begin," I said. "We have so much to catch up on, and you have so many pressing cares."

"None that are more important than you right now," he said. "I missed you every day we were apart. Is that what is bothering you? Have you left someone behind?"

By someone, he meant someone *male*. "No, Llywelyn. I didn't marry again. I couldn't."

"I imagine you had suitors ..." his voice trailed off and I smiled. He didn't want to ask but I saw no reason not to tell him the truth.

"You would be disappointed in the men of the twenty-first century if they hadn't chased after me, wouldn't you?"

I had him there. "I would."

"None could compare to you," I said, "and so none lasted. I had my work and my children."

"And that was enough?"

"It was never enough." I sighed. "But that's not what you asked about." I pushed to my feet and pulled a stool closer to him so my face was more level with his. "And that's not what I need to tell you about."

"Did something ... *happen* to you on your journey here?"

Fear resounded in his voice, but I put a hand on his knee, anxious to reassure him that he was far off the mark. "No, Llywelyn. But I did have an encounter with a man, one who used to serve your brother, Dafydd."

This was not what he'd been expecting. "What was his name?"

"Marc," I said. "He and the prioress at the convent shared a father, Evan, who served you once upon a time, during a fight with Roger Mortimer in Powys."

Llywelyn shook his head. "I have no memory of the man."

"Well, the son was in your brother's *teulu*, and you probably remember him. He was at Dafydd's right hand all through the year I was with you, and in all the years since. Dafydd dismissed him only this spring."

Llywelyn gazed into the fire, his eyes narrowing as he thought. "I do know of this man—of course I do. And it was in the spring that I noticed that Marc was no longer in attendance on Dafydd. Why does this concern you?"

"Because Marc spoke of a plot against you—or perhaps against our son." I then related the whole story of my meeting with Marc, what he'd said to me about his dismissal being *my* fault, and the exchange on the road with Henry. "Marc used the words, *the Prince*, when he was speaking about the failed plot. At the time, I didn't know David was here so I assumed he meant you. Marc fled in its aftermath and your brother was concerned enough that he might talk about it—betray him—that he sent men to track him down. I was with Marc when Henry found him."

Llywelyn rubbed his chin with his right hand. "Did you say Henry?"

I nodded.

"That man is a snake."

"So it seemed to me," I said. "He certainly was out for Marc's blood, and all the worse because they're brothers too."

"Do you know any more details of what they planned than this?"

I shook my head. "I'm sorry, my lord. I don't."

Llywelyn took in a deep breath and let it out. "I know of no plot against me or against our son. I don't trust my brother, of course, but he has been loyal—almost to a fault—of late."

"That's what I understood," I said. "But I had to tell you."

"What I don't understand is why Marc blamed you for his downfall."

"He never made that clear. Thinking back, I'd guess your brother's plot was against David, and I would have to agree that David's existence is my fault. Your brother must feel enormous resentment against our son for taking his place as your heir. By extension, he must resent me."

Llywelyn laughed. "Did I ever tell you what Dafydd said about you, right before we swept through Caerphilly?"

I shook my head.

"He said that you had quite a mouth on you."

I smiled, as I knew he wanted.

Llywelyn laughed again. "He's never had any real idea of what love is, or why you are so important to me." He turned serious again, gazing into my eyes. And then he leaned forward and cupped my face in his hands. "I missed you. Your honesty, your uprightness, your beauty. I see you in our precious children. Thank you for them. Thank you for returning to me."

I felt myself falling into him, falling in love with him all over again, as if the years we'd lost had never happened. His arms came around me.

"I spent sixteen years trying to find my way back to you," I said.

"I know. I looked for you every day, everywhere I went. We need to make sure that none of you lose your way in time again."

"I don't know how to do that, Llywelyn. I don't know *why* I ever came here in the first place."

"I do." Llywelyn eased back so he could look into my face. "You came to save me. And you have."

Thank you for reading *Winds of Time*. All of the books in the *After Cilmeri* series are available at any bookstore. For more information about dark age and medieval Wales, please see my web page: www.sarahwoodbury.com

About the Author

With two historian parents, Sarah couldn't help but develop an interest in the past. She went on to get more than enough education herself (in anthropology) and began writing fiction when the stories in her head overflowed and demanded she let them out. While her ancestry is Welsh, she only visited Wales for the first time while in college. She has been in love with the country, language, and people ever since. She even convinced her husband to give all four of their children Welsh names.

She makes her home in Oregon.

www.sarahwoodbury.com

30163580R00061

Made in the USA
Lexington, KY
07 February 2019